Words to Know Before

claws

dinosaur

glop

jungle

sticky

swish

teeth

www.rourkeeducationalmedia.com

Edited by Precious McKenzie
Illustrated by Ed Myer
Art Direction and Page Layout by Renee Brady

Library of Congress PCN Data

We're Going on a Dinosaur Dig / Anastasia Suen
ISBN 978-1-61810-166-2 (hard cover) (alk. paper)
ISBN 978-1-61810-299-7 (soft cover)
Library of Congress Control Number: 2012936768

Also Available as:

Scan for Related Titles
and Teacher Resources

Rourke Educational Media
Printed in the United States of America,
North Mankato, Minnesota

rourkeeducationalmedia.com

customerservice@rourkeeducationalmedia.com • PO Box 643328 Vero Beach, Florida 32964

We're Going on a DINOSAUR DIG

By Anastasia Suen

Illustrated by Ed Myer

We're going on a dinosaur dig.

We're going to find a big one.
Here we go!

Oh no!
Grass!
Tall, tall grass!

Here we go!
Swish, swish!
Swish, swish!

We're going on a dinosaur dig.

We're going to find a big one.
Here we go!

Oh no!
Mud!
Sticky, sticky mud!

Here we go!
Glop, glop!
Glop, glop!

We're going on a dinosaur dig.

We're going to find a big one.
Here we go!

Oh no!
A jungle!
A dark, dark jungle!

Here we go!

Trip, ouch!

Trip, ouch!

I see a long tail.
I see big claws.
I see sharp teeth.

A dinosaur!
Oh no!
It's alive!
Run!

Here we go!
Back through the jungle.
Trip, ouch!
Trip, ouch!

Here we go!
Back through the mud.
Glop, glop!
Glop, glop!

Here we go!
Back through the grass.
Swish, swish!
Swish, swish!

Close the door! Close the door!
ROAR!

After Reading Activities

You and the Story...

Can you name the places the children went?

What did they find?

Have you ever taken a walk?

What did you see?

Words You Know Now...

Many big words have little words in them. Write the words listed below on a sheet of paper and then circle the little words that you find in them. Example: dinosaur (circle 'no').

claws	sticky
dinosaur	swish
glop	teeth
jungle	

You Could...Go for a Walk with Your Family and Friends

- Decide on a safe route for your walk.

- Bring a camera or bring a notebook and pencil.

- Write or draw the things you find on your walk.

About the Author

Anastasia Suen lives with her family in Plano, Texas. When her children were small they went on many dinosaur digs, but they never found a live dinosaur.

Meet The Author!
www.meetREMauthors.com

About the Illustrator

Ed Myer is a Manchester-born illustrator now living in London. After growing up in an artistic household, Ed studied ceramics at university but always continued drawing pictures. As well as illustration, Ed likes traveling, playing computer games, and walking little Ted (his Jack Russell).